The Bartokk Assassins

GAME BOOK

The galaxy is yours.
Be a part of

E P I S O D E I
ADVENTURES

#1 Search for the Lost Jedi
#2 The Bartokk Assassins
#3 The Fury of Darth Maul

. . . and more to come!

STAR WARS®

EPISODE I

ADVENTURES

GAME BOOK

The Bartokk Assassins

No part of this publication may be reproduced in whole or in part, or stored in a retrieval system, or transmitted in any form or by any means, electronic, mechanical, photocopying, recording, or otherwise, without written permission of the publisher. For information regarding permission, write to Scholastic Inc., Attention: Permissions Department, 555 Broadway, New York, NY 10012.

ISBN 0-439-12985-0

SCHOLASTIC and the associated logos are trademarks and/or registered trademarks of Scholastic Inc.

12 11 10 9 8 7 6 5 4 3 2 1   9/9 0/0 01 02 03 04

Printed in the U.S.A.

First Scholastic printing, December 1999

SCHOLASTIC INC.

New York Toronto London Auckland Sydney
Mexico City New Delhi Hong Kong

ISBN 0-439-12985-0

12 11 10 9 8 7 6 5 4 3 2 1   9/9 0 1 2 3 4/0

Printed in the U.S.A.
First Scholastic printing, October 1999

The Bartokk Assassins
GAME BOOK

YOUR ADVENTURE BEGINS!

For the full story behind your adventure, read up to page 32 in your Star Wars Adventures novel, *The Bartokk Assassins*. Or begin here.

You are a Jedi, Bama Vook, or the droid Leeper. The *Adventure Guide* contains the rules of *Star Wars Adventures*. You must follow these rules at all times.

The Bartokk assassins have reclaimed their freighter. Their ship contains Trade Federation droid starfighters and a Neimoidian hyperdrive engine. The Bartokks have also abducted Bama Vook's son Chup-Chup. You must battle the Bartokks on Esseles. After you defeat them, you will pursue their freighter. To prevent the Bartokks from carrying out their mission, you must board the freighter, learn its destination, and retrieve the Neimoidian prototype hyperdrive engine. Most importantly, you must rescue Chup-Chup from the Bartokks. After accomplishing these goals, you will attempt to destroy the Bartokk freighter along with its cargo of droid starfighters. This will not be an easy task.

3

There are fifteen Bartokks in every assassin team. Two Bartokks have already been eliminated. You will encounter the remaining thirteen Bartokks in this adventure. At least three Bartokks remain on Esseles, but there may be more. Keep careful count of the Bartokks during this adventure so you will know how many you will encounter on their freighter.

Choose your character. Every character has unique talents that are listed on each character card.

Bama Vook and Leeper cannot use Jedi Power, but they can use their own power and talents (indicated on the back of their character cards). Bama Vook is exceptionally strong and has a keen sense of smell; Leeper is skilled at repairs and his spring-loaded legs enable him to jump very high. Both Bama and Leeper know how to handle a blaster.

You can take no more than three devices and one vehicle (it must be capable of space travel) on this adventure. You can use Power three times on this adventure.

You start this adventure with your Adventure Point (AP) total from your previous adventure, or 1000 AP if this is your first adventure.

May the Force be with you.

YOUR ADVENTURE:

THE BARTOKK
ASSASSINS

The Three Bartokks seem to have you and your allies cornered near the lift tube at Docking Bay 28. One false move and the assassins will shoot their arrows.

From your position, you can hear the rumble of the Bartokk freighter's engine within the docking bay. The assassins have taken Chup-Chup as a hostage, and you doubt they have any intention of releasing him. Bartokks do not have a reputation for letting hostages survive.

As your eyes remain on the three assassins you pick up a flickering movement in your peripheral vision: a shadow glides across the outer wall of the docking bay across the street. The shadow is cast by something directly above you, and you look up in time to see a wide stun net dropping from the roof. In that instant, you realize the three Bartokks on the ground were a distraction — a fourth assassin has sprung a trap.

Stun nets carry an electric charge that is capable of knocking out organic creatures as well as droids. There isn't any time to warn your friends.

Choose to duck inside an empty cargo crate or dive under the landspeeder.

To duck inside an empty cargo crate: Roll the 10-dice to slip into the crate before the net can snag you. The number you roll is your roll#. Your roll# + your stealth# is your adventure#.

If your adventure# is equal to or more than 6, add the difference to your AP total. You move so fast, the Bartokks don't see you duck inside the crate as the net falls on your comrads. (Only Trinkatta — who you can see under the landspeeder — is safe.) You may proceed.

If your adventure# is less than 6, subtract the difference from your AP total. The crate only appeared to be empty, but is actually filled with thick sheets of transparisteel. There isn't any room for you to hide. Proceed to dive under the landspeeder (below).

To dive under the landspeeder: Roll the 20-dice to jump through the air and slide underneath the parked speeder. The number you roll is your roll#. Your roll# + your stealth# + your strength# is your adventure#.

If your adventure# is equal to or more than 12, add the difference to your AP total. You dive and roll next to the cowering Trinkatta as the net lands on your unprepared friends. The Bartokks didn't see your quick dive and you may proceed.

If your adventure# is less than 12, subtract the difference from your AP total. You misjudged the distance of your jump and your shoulder smashes into the side of the landspeeder. Roll the 20-dice again to scramble under the landspeeder. Your new roll# + your stealth# + 1 is your new adventure#.

> *If your new adventure# is equal to or more than 11,* add the difference to your AP total. Under the landspeeder, Trinkatta is startled to see you suddenly lying next to him. You raise a finger to your lips, cautioning him to remain silent. The Bartokks don't yet realize you have escaped the net. You may proceed.

> *If your new adventure# is less than 11,* subtract the difference from your AP total. Trinkatta drags you under the landspeeder — just in time. You may proceed.

The moment the dropped stun net touches your friends, its adhesive duracord strands wrap around their bodies, pinning them to each other. All the strands suddenly glow a bright white-blue, and a powerful electric surge is unleashed to knock out the captives. There is nothing you can do to help. The surge ends with a fizzling sound, and the unconscious victims tumble to the ground in a snared heap.

From your hiding place, you watch the three assassins on the street. You can't see the one on the roof. It would be suicide to attack three Bartokks. You wait to make your move.

At the same time, the three Bartokks relax their grips on their crossbows and take one step closer to the stun net. With their hive mind, the insectoid creatures move in the same fashion, like puppets controlled by a single brain.

Your mind races. You wonder if the Bartokks realize that two of their targets escaped the stun net. Will they leave for the freighter or search for you and Trinkatta? Will you be able to board their freighter and accomplish your goals without anyone getting killed?

Each of the three Bartokks reaches to his backpack and retrieves a spear. Then they raise the spears, preparing to bring them down on the defenseless bodies within the stun net.

The Bartokk who threw the stun net is still not visible. But unless you move now, your friends will perish.

Choose to fight the Bartokks or use Power to disarm them. If you choose to fight the Bartokks, choose to fight them all at once or one at a time.

To disarm the Bartokks (using Power)*:
Choose your Confusion Power. Roll the 20-dice to make each of the three Bartokks think the other two are his mortal enemies, using either the Force or your own verbal skill. Your roll# + your power# + your Power's high-resist# is your adventure#.

If your adventure# is equal to or more than 13, add the difference to your AP total. Each of the three Bartokks believes he will perish unless he shoots his arrows at the other two. The three assassins release their poison-tipped arrows at the same time, and each arrow finds its mark. All three Bartokks are out of commission before they hit the ground. You may proceed.

If your adventure# is less than 13, subtract the difference from your AP total. Worried about your unconscious friends, you are unable to concentrate your Power on the Bartokks. Proceed to fight the Bartokks all at once (below).

*NOTE: This counts as one of three Power uses you are allowed on this adventure.

To fight the Bartokks all at once: Choose a weapon. Roll the 10-dice to target the chemical waste storage container in front of Docking Bay 27. Your roll# + your weaponry# + your weapon's far-ranged# is your adventure#.

If your adventure# is equal to or more than 8, add the difference to your AP total. You fire a hole into the chemical waste storage container. The tank explodes, spraying toxic chemical waste onto the three Bartokks. The Bartokks and their weapons are liquified and you may proceed.

If your adventure# is less than 8, subtract the difference from your AP total. You missed the storage tank. Proceed to fight the Bartokks one at a time (below).

To fight the Bartokks one at a time: Choose your weapon. Roll the 10-dice to battle the nearest Bartokk. Your roll# + your weaponry# + your weapon's mid-range# is your adventure#.

If your adventure# is equal to or more than 8, add the difference to your AP total. One Bartokk is defeated. Go back to the phrase *To fight the Bartokks one at a time* and repeat. If you defeat a second Bartokk, go back to "Roll the 10-dice to battle the nearest Bartokk" and repeat. When you have defeated three Bartokks, you may proceed.

If your adventure# is less than 8, subtract the difference from your AP total. You have only wounded a Bartokk and it continues to attack. Roll the 20-dice to terminate the assassin. Your new roll# + your weaponry# + your weapon's mid-range# + 1 is your new adventure#.

If your new adventure# is equal to or more than 13, add 2 AP to your AP total. The Bartokk is finally felled by your weapon. If you have not yet defeated all three Bartokks, go back to "Roll the 20-dice to terminate the assassin" and repeat. When all three Bartokk's are defeated, you may proceed.

If your new adventure# is less than 13, subtract the difference from your AP total. The Bartokk is an unrelenting and unforgiving opponent. Go back to "Roll the 20-dice to terminate the assassin" and repeat. When all three Bartokks are defeated, you may proceed.

As the three Bartokks are struck down, their arrows and spears scatter across the ground.

You have single-handedly defeated three Bartokk assassins. Add 75 AP to your AP total.

An ear-piercing shriek sounds from above, and you glance up in time to see a single Bartokk perched at the curved edge of the roof. It's the Bartokk who threw the stun net, and he's furious because you defeated three members of his hive. The Bartokk pulls a broad-bladed gutting knife from his weapons belt and springs out into the air, descending headfirst in a murderous dive.

Choose to dodge or fight the Bartokk assassin. If you choose to fight, choose to fight with a Bartokk spear or one of your own weapons.

To dodge the Bartokk: Roll the 10-dice to jump away from the plummeting assassin. Your roll# + your stealth# + 1 is your adventure#.

If your adventure# is equal to or more than 7, add the difference to your AP total. You successfully dodge the Bartokk. He smashes headlong into the ground and is knocked out. You may proceed.

If your adventure# is less than 7, subtract the difference from your AP total. You manage to step aside but the Bartokk coils his body and executes a perfect dive-forward to come up standing. The insectoid alien gnashes his mandibles at you. Proceed to fight the Bartokk with a spear or one of your own weapons (below).

To fight the Bartokk assassin with a Bartokk spear: Roll the 20-dice to snatch a spear from a dead Bartokk and aim it at the diving assassin. Your roll# + your stealth# + your strength# is your adventure#.

If your adventure# is equal to or more than 15, add the difference to your AP total. Grabbing the spear, you quickly angle its sharp end up in the air, aiming it straight at the descending Bartokk. The diving assassin lands on the spear and is killed. You may proceed.

If your adventure# is less than 15, subtract the difference from your AP total. The Bartokk narrowly misses the spear and lands on the ground. He turns to attack you with his knife. Roll the 20-dice again to hurl the spear at the knife-wielding Bartokk. Your new roll# + your weaponry# + your strength# + 2 is your new adventure#.

> *If your new adventure# is equal to or more than 15,* add the difference to your AP total. You pin the Bartokk to the outer wall of Docking Bay 28. The assassin is defeated and you may proceed.

> *If your new adventure# is less than 15,* subtract the difference from your AP total. You hurl the spear but the Bartokk snatches it in mid-air. Twirling the spear in one of his clawlike hands, the Bartokk makes a rapid chittering sound. You can't tell from his insectoid features, but you get the impression that the assassin is laughing at your failed effort to strike him down. Suddenly, he leaps at you with both the knife and spear. Proceed to fight the Bartokk with one of your own weapons (next page).

To fight the Bartokk with one of your own weapons: Choose your weapon. Roll the 10-dice to battle the leaping assassin. Your roll# + your weaponry# + your weapon's mid-range# is your adventure#.

If your adventure# is equal to or more than 10, add the difference to your AP total. The Bartokk is defeated and you may proceed.

If your adventure# is less than 10, subtract 5 AP from your AP total. The leaping assassin knocks your weapon from your grip before he lands. The foul-smelling Bartokk is practically on top of you! You grab a poisoned-tip arrow from the leather quiver at his back. Roll the 20-dice to jab the Bartokk. Your new roll# + your stealth# + 1 is your new adventure#.

If your new adventure# is equal to or more than 14, add the difference to your AP total. In a single sweeping movement, you snatch the arrow from the Bartokk's quiver and ram it through his armor-plated arm. The poison takes immediate effect and the brutal creature collapses at your feet. You may proceed.

If your new adventure# is less than 14, subtract the difference from your AP total. The

Bartokk is putting up an incredible fight. Go back to "Roll the 20-dice to jab the Bartokk" and repeat. When the Bartokk is defeated, you may proceed.

On the fallen Bartokk's weapons belt, you see what appears to be a remote control unit for the stun net. You grab the control unit and run to your unconscious allies.

The roar of a large repulsorlift engine again fills the air. You look up to see the spike-covered Bartokk freighter rise up and away from Docking Bay 28. Although the Bartokks might have been delaying their lift off in anticipation of a victory over you and your friends, it seems they have decided to abandon their dead and make their escape.

The Bartokk freighter is a massive vessel, nearly seventy meters long and twenty-five meters wide. It is organic in appearance, resembling a bloated, barb-encrusted sea creature. Even the large, triangular sensor dish that juts out from one side of the vessel looks more like a fin than a technical extension. On the freighter's other side, a six-winged Bartokk star-fighter is moored to the outer hull, looking like a mutant offspring clinging to its gargantuan mother.

Because the freighter is not equipped with a hyperdrive engine, it will take several minutes for it to reach the upper stratosphere of Esseles and enter space. You decide to use this time to free your unconscious friends from the stun net.

Although the stun net is no longer releasing any electric surge, its duracord strands are locked tightly around your allies. You aren't certain how to operate the Bartokk-designed remote control unit, but it should be the easiest way to release the stun net. Closely examining the net, you believe you could also use a lightsaber to carefully cut a hole through the duracord strands.

Choose to deactivate the stun net or cut through the stun net with a lightsaber.

To deactivate the stun net: Roll the 10-dice to switch off the Bartokk net. Your roll# + your knowledge# + your skill# is your adventure#.

If your adventure# is equal to or more than 8, add the difference to your AP total. After you press a switch on the control unit, the net instantly loosens and slides off of your unconscious friends. You may proceed.

If your adventure# is less than 8, subtract 10 AP from your AP total. You touched the wrong switch! The switch unleashes a powerful shock your way. Roll the 10-dice again to depress the same switch and end the electric surge. Your new roll# + your skill# minus 1 is your new adventure#.

If your new adventure# is equal to or more than 7, add 2 AP to your AP total. You end the electric surge. Cautious of pushing another wrong switch, you set the Bartokk control unit aside. Recovering from the shock, you must proceed to cut through the stun net with a lightsaber (next page).

If your new adventure# is less than 7, subtract the difference from your AP total. You pressed the switch too hard and the electric surge becomes more powerful. Go back to "Roll the 10-dice again to depress the same switch and end the electric surge" and repeat. When you deactivate the stun net, you must recover from the shock. Proceed to cut through it with a lightsaber (next page).

To cut through the stun net with a lightsaber: If you are Bama Vook or Leeper, you can reach through the net and borrow a lightsaber from one of the unconscious Jedi. Roll the 20-dice to use a lightsaber. If you are recovering from a shock, your hands are pretty shaky and your roll# + your weapon# + your weaponry# + your weapon's close-range# −2 is your adventure#. If you haven't been shocked trying to deactivate the stun net, your roll# + your weaponry# + your weapon's close-range# is your adventure#.

If your adventure# is equal to or more than 13, add the difference to your AP total. You carefully slice through the metal strands, then remove the ruined stun net from the unconscious figures. You may proceed.

If your adventure# is less than 13, subtract the difference from your AP total. You are nervous about using a lightsaber in such close proximity to your unconscious friends. You must remain calm. Roll the 20-dice again to remain calm. If calm is one of your talents, your new roll# + your weaponry# + your weapon's close-range# + your knowledge# is your new adventure#. If calm is not one of your talents, your new roll# + your weaponry# + your weapon's close-range# + 1 is your new adventure#.

If your new adventure# is equal to or more than 15, add 3 AP to your AP total. Remaining calm, you slice through the stun net and remove it from the unconscious figures. You may proceed.

If your new adventure# is less than 15, subtract the difference from your AP total. Go back to "Roll the 20-dice again to remain calm" and repeat. After you have cut through the stun net and removed it from your allies, you may proceed.

As you pull the stun net away from your unconscious friends, Trinkatta slithers out from under the parked landspeeder. "Is it over?" he asks. "Are our friends all right?"

"They'll be fine," you answer. "They just need some time to recover." One at a time, you carefully lift and place each unconscious body within the landspeeder.

For saving your friends, reward yourself 70 AP.

"I'm sorry I wasn't any help," Trinkatta sighs. "When I saw those Bartokks, I was paralyzed with fear!"

"Then here's your chance to help," you

24

remark. "Take the landspeeder back to your factory. Until they wake up, our friends here need someone to watch over and protect them. They need *you*, Trinkatta."

"But . . . why can't *you* watch them?" Trinkatta asks nervously.

"That Bartokk freighter's carrying the Trade Federation's starfighters and hyperdrive engine," you reply. "I'm going after it."

"By yourself?" Trinkatta gasps as you pick him up and deposit him behind the controls of the speeder.

"The Bartokks have a hostage," you remind the Kloodavian. "They must be stopped. The *Metron Burner* should still be in Docking Bay 28. If it's in one piece, I'll use it to fly after the freighter."

"But think of the odds you're up against," Trinkatta warns. "How many Bartokks are left? I've lost track."

"Don't worry about it — just wish me luck," you suggest. "Now get moving!"

As Trinkatta starts the speeder, you notice two hooded figures lurking across the street. You're not certain, but they look like two Neimoidians. It's possible they heard your conversation with Trinkatta about the freighter's cargo, but you don't have time to deal with them now. Trinkatta zooms down the street with his three passengers, and you run to the lift tube to Docking Bay 28.

You press a switch but the lift does not descend. Something is wrong with the lift mechanism.

To reach the starship *Metron Burner,* choose to repair the lift tube controls, create a hole through the lift tube floor, or climb over the docking bay wall. If you choose to create a hole through the lift tube floor, you then must choose to jump or climb down to the bottom of the lift tube.

To repair the lift tube controls: Roll the 10-dice to fix the controls that will allow you to descend into the docking bay. If repair is one of your talents, your roll# + your knowledge# + your skill# + 1 is your adventure#. If repair is not one of your talents, your roll# + your skill# is your adventure#.

If your adventure# is equal to or more than 8, add the difference to your AP total. Fixing the controls is an easy task. You reconnect a frayed wire and the lift descends through the tube. You reach the lower interior of the docking bay and may proceed.

If your adventure# is less than 8, subtract the difference from your AP total. You receive a shock from a frayed wire, and the controls are fried. Proceed to create a hole through the lift tube floor (below).

To create a hole through the lift tube floor: Choose your weapon. Roll the 20-dice to use your weapon to make an opening in the floor that's large enough for you to pass through. Your roll# + your weaponry# + your weapon's close-range# is your adventure#.

If your adventure# is equal to or more than 14, add the difference to your AP total. You manage to punch a large hole through the floor. Choose to climb or jump down to the bottom of the lift tube (next page).

If your adventure# is less than 14, subtract 7 AP from your AP total. Although you created an opening in the lift tube floor, it's too small for you to fit through. Roll the 20-dice again to widen the hole in the floor. Your new roll# + your weaponry# + your weapon's close-range# + 1 is your new adventure#.

If your new adventure# is equal to or more than 15, add the difference to your AP total. You have successfully enlarged the opening in the floor. Choose to climb or jump down to the bottom of the lift tube (below).

If your new adventure# is less than 15, subtract the difference from your AP total. Either the lift tube floor is made of heavily reinforced material, or you could use some more practice with your weapon. You abandon the lift tube. Proceed to climb over the docking bay wall (next page).

To climb down to the bottom of the lift tube: Roll the 10-dice to grab hold of a wall-mounted energy cable and climb down the lift tube shaft. You must have already cut through the lift tube floor in order to do this. Your roll# + your strength# + 2 is your adventure#.

If your adventure# is equal to or more than 9, add the difference to your AP total. Keeping a tight grip on the cable, you plant your feet against the walls of the lift tube and quickly descend to the docking bay floor. You may proceed.

If your adventure# is less than 9, subtract the difference from your AP total. You lose your grip on the cable! Proceed to jump down to the bottom of the lift tube (below).

To jump down to the bottom of the lift tube: Roll the 10-dice to leap from the lift to the base of the shaft. If jumping is one of your talents, your roll# + your strength# + 2 is your adventure#. If jumping is not one of your talents, your roll# + your strength# is your adventure#.

If your adventure# is equal to or more than 8, add the difference to your AP total. You land safely at the bottom of the shaft. You may proceed.

If your adventure# is less than 8, subtract 20 AP from your AP total. You land hard — you're lucky to be alive. You have hurt your leg. Keep this in mind as you proceed — you may have to subtract from your adventure# later on.

To climb over the docking bay wall: Roll the 20-dice to scale the four-story outer wall of Docking Bay 28. Your roll# + your stealth# + your strength# is your adventure#.

If your adventure# is equal to or more than 14, add the difference to your AP total. You scramble up and over the docking bay wall faster than a Kowakian monkey-lizard. You reach the interior of Docking Bay 28 and proceed.

If your adventure# is less than 14, subtract the difference from your AP total. You succeed in climbing up and over the docking bay wall, but when you land within the bay, you hear a beeping sound. You have activated the security system! Above your position, a small laser cannon springs out from a roof-mounted turret and snaps into position to shoot at you. You must destroy the laser cannon before it fires. Choose your weapon. Roll the 10-dice to destroy the small laser cannon. If defense is one of your talents, your new roll# + your weaponry# + your weapon's far-range# + 2 is your new adventure#. If defense is not one of your talents, your new roll# + your weaponry# + your weapon's far-range# is your new adventure#.

If your new adventure# is equal to or more than 10, add the difference to your AP total. The laser cannon blows up. You may proceed.

If your adventure# is less than 10, subtract the difference from your AP total. The laser canon fires, nearly hitting you and carving out a chunk of stone near your feet before you are able to draw your own weapon. Go back to "Roll the 10-dice to destroy the small laser cannon" and repeat. When you have blown up the laser cannon, you may proceed.

There are two starships within Docking Bay 28. The larger ship is a Corellian YT-1300 Transport. The smaller ship is a Z-95 Headhunter, modified to carry two pilots and capable of space travel. The YT-1300 has a greater carrying capacity, but the Headhunter is probably much faster. Both ships look like they're in good shape.

The Bartokk freighter is no longer within view. You can't afford to lose any more time.

After selecting a starship, you climb into the cockpit and prepare to lift off. To reach space, choose to launch using the auto-pilot or the manual controls.

To launch using the autopilot: Choose your vehicle (it must be capable of space travel). Roll the 10-dice to activate the autopilot for a smooth lift off. Your roll# + your navigation# −1 is your adventure#.

If your adventure# is equal to or more than 6, add the difference to your AP total. Guided by the autopilot controls, your starship rises up and away from Docking Bay 28. In less than a minute, you leave Esseles' ionosphere and enter space. You may proceed.

If your adventure# is less than 6, subtract the difference from your AP total. The autopilot functions are taking too long to come online. Proceed to launch using the manual controls (below).

To launch using the manual controls: Choose your vehicle (it must be capable of space travel). Roll the 10-dice to lift off. If navigation is one of your talents, your roll# + your navigation# + 2 is your adventure#. If navigation is not one of your talents, your roll# + your navigation# + 1 is your adventure#.

If your adventure# is equal to or more than 9, add the difference to your AP total. You steer your starship up and out of Docking Bay 28, and you quickly ascend through Esseles' atmosphere until you enter space. You may proceed.

If your adventure# is less than 9, subtract the difference from your AP total. While your starship remains on the ground, a loud beeping sound fills the cockpit. To prevent anyone from pursuing them, the Bartokks planted a bomb under your seat! By initiating the repulsorlift, you have activated a timer mechanism. You must deactivate the bomb or your entire star-ship will explode. Roll the 20-dice to deactivate the bomb. If repair is one of your talents, your new roll# + your knowledge# + your skill# + 2 is your new adventure#. If repair is not one of your talents, your new roll# + your knowl-edge# + your skill# is your new adventure#.

If your new adventure# is equal to or more than 14, add the difference to your AP to-tal. The bomb turns out to be a simple pro-ton grenade, and you deactivate it without any difficulty. Unfortunately, you must still lift off from Docking Bay 28. Go back to "Roll the 10-dice to lift off" and repeat un-til you have blasted away from Esseles. Then you may proceed.

If your new adventure# is less than 14, sub-tract the difference from your AP total. Go back to "Roll the 20-dice to deactivate the bomb" and repeat.

Entering space, you gaze outside the cockpit canopy, only to see a field of stars. Even without a hyperdrive engine, the Bar-tokk freighter is already beyond visual range of Esseles. To locate the Bartokk freighter, choose to use Power or your starship's scan-mode sensors.

To locate the Bartokk freighter (using Power)*: Choose your Find Power. Roll the 20-dice to find the fleeing freighter amidst the stars. Your roll# + your Power# + your Power's mid-resist# is your adventure#.

If your adventure# is equal to or more than 12, add the difference to your AP total. The Bartokks emit a distinct wave of menace across space. You angle your ship after the freighter and proceed.

If your adventure# is less than 12, subtract the difference from your AP total. Perhaps the Bartokks are able to block your sensory powers. You might do better to focus your powers on the abducted Chup-Chup. Closing your eyes, you concentrate. Roll the 20-dice. Your new roll# + your power# + 4 is your new adventure#.

If your new adventure# is equal to or more than 15, add the difference to your AP total. The captured Chup-Chup's fear is an unmistakable beacon through space. Although you wish he were not so afraid, you are somewhat reassured to know the young

Talz is still alive. You adjust your controls to pursue the freighter and proceed.

If your new adventure# is less than 15, subtract the difference from your AP total. You are unable to sense the whereabouts of Chup-Chup. Proceed to locate the Bartokk freighter using your starship's scan-mode sensors (below).

*NOTE: This counts as one of three Power uses you are allowed on this adventure.

To locate the Bartokk freighter using your starship's scan-mode sensors: Roll the 10-dice to scan a broad area of space around Esseles. Your roll# + your skill# is your adventure#.

If your adventure# is equal to or more than 7, add the difference to your AP total. A blinking blip appears on your scanner grid. It is the fleeing freighter. You adjust your path of flight to follow the Bartokks' ship. You may proceed.

If your adventure# is less than 7, subtract 3 AP from your AP total. Your scan-mode sensors are jammed. Despite what any flight instructor has ever told you, you know that a sticky sensor can become unstuck by a single swift whack. Roll the 10-dice again to smack your fist down on the scanner console. Your new roll# + your strength# + is your new adventure#.

If your new adventure# is equal to or more than 7, add the difference to your AP total. Your flight instructor would surely frown, but your fist manages to bring the scan-mode sensors online. The Bartokk freighter appears as a blip on the screen. Veering to follow the freighter, you may proceed.

If your new adventure# is less than 7, subtract the difference from your AP total. You brought your fist down too hard and broke the scan-mode sensor, which is precisely why your flight instructor warned you about trying this. You must repair the scan-mode sensor. Roll the 20-dice to fix the broken sensor unit. If repair is one of your talents, your new roll# + your knowledge# + your skill# + 2 is your new adventure#. If repair is not one of your talents, your new roll# + your knowledge# + your skill# is your new adventure#.

If your new adventure# is equal to or more than 15, add the difference to your AP total. You repair the scan-mode sensors and the Bartokk freighter appears as a blip on the scanner grid. Angling after the freighter, you may proceed.

If your new adventure# is less than 15, subtract the difference from your AP total. Go back to "Roll the 20-dice to fix the broken sensor unit" and repeat. After you have repaired the unit, the Bartokk freighter is located and you may proceed.

In order to speed across space and catch up with the Bartokk freighter, you must initiate your vehicle's drive system.

To initiate the drive system: Roll the 10-dice to make your vehicle accelerate. Your roll# + your vehicle's speed# + your vehicle's distance# is your adventure#.

If your adventure# is equal to or more than 9, add the difference to your AP total. Your vehicle blasts through space at incredible speed. You may proceed.

If your adventure# is less than 9, subtract the difference from your AP total. Your vehicle's powerful thrusters propel you faster than you'd anticipated, and the gravitational force crushes you back against your seat. Unless you can adjust your acceleration compensator, you won't be able to neutralize the devastating effects of high-speed maneuvering. It will take all your strength to reach the controls. Roll the 20-dice to reach the acceleration compensator. If strength is one of your talents, your new roll# + your strength# + 2 is your new adventure#. If strength is not one of your talents, your new roll# + your strength# is your new adventure#.

If your new adventure# is equal to or more than 12, add 3 AP to your AP total. You reach the acceleration compensator and adjust the artificial gravity within your vehicle. Your vehicle continues to race through space and you may proceed.

If your new adventure# is less than 12, subtract 3 AP from your AP total. Your hand almost grasps the controls. Go back to "Roll the 20-dice to reach the acceleration compensator" and repeat. After you have successfully adjusted the artificial gravity within your vehicle, you may proceed.

Soaring through space, you leave the planet Esseles behind and head for the fleeing Bartokk freighter. Thoughts of the helpless young Chup-Chup enter your mind, but you push them aside. All you can do is hope the Bartokks haven't caused him any harm, and maintain your determination to rescue him.

The Bartokk freighter comes into view. Ignoring spacer protocol, the Bartokks have switched off their running lights so their freighter appears as a dark blot against the starfield. If it weren't for the distinctive silhouette of the triangular sensor dish, you might have mistaken the freighter for a large meteor.

An alarm sounds and a red light flashes within your starship's cockpit. You have accidentally flown within the freighter's sensor range. The freighter's running lights suddenly illuminate.

The Bartokks know you have arrived.

As you ponder your next move, you see a small engine flare at the side of the freighter. It's the six-winged Bartokk fighter craft, and its coming straight at you.

Bartokk starfighters require a crew of three: a pilot, a gunner, and a tailgunner. You have never actually seen the interior of such a fighter, but diagrams have revealed that the each of the three Bartokks should be positioned with their backs to one another while each assassin has a view out a triangular viewport. Because the Bartokks communicate telepathically and share a hive mind, they function as a single twelve-armed pilot.

The Bartokk fighter fires a proton torpedo. The explosive warhead races toward your ship. Choose to evade the proton torpedo, deploy an ion mine, or blast the proton torpedo.

To evade the proton torpedo: Roll the 20-dice to veer away from the oncoming warhead. If navigation is one of your talents, your roll# + your navigation# + your vehicle's stealth# + 2 is your adventure#. If navigation is not one of your talents, your roll# + your navigation# + your vehicle's stealth# is your adventure#.

If your adventure# is equal to or more than 13, add the difference to your AP total. As you bank hard and away from the proton torpedo, it streaks past your starship. Seconds later, it explodes in the distance. You may proceed.

If your adventure# is less than 13, subtract the difference from your AP total. The proton torpedo zooms past you, but instead of detonating, it loops back in pursuit of your starship. The torpedo has a built-in homing sensor that's tracking your flight path. Roll the 20-dice again to fly directly toward the Bartokk starfighter. Your new roll# + your navigation# + your vehicle's speed# + 2 is your new adventure#.

If your new adventure# is equal to or more than 15, add 2 AP to your AP total. The Bartokks realize you're trying to draw the proton torpedo dangerously close to their own starfighter. Hoping to prevent sudden death, one of the Bartokk gunners triggers the proton torpedo with a remote control unit, causing it to blow up before it can reach his starfighter, or yours. You imagine the Bartokks must feel foolish for wasting the torpedo. You may proceed.

If your new adventure# is less than 15, subtract 2 AP from your AP total. The Bartokk starfighter takes evasive action and flies out of range from your ship. The proton torpedo is closing in on you! Proceed to deploy an ion mine (below).

To deploy an ion mine: Roll the 10-dice to release a powerful ion mine from your starship. Your roll# + your vehicle's weaponry# is your adventure#.

If your adventure# is equal to or more than 6, add the difference to your AP total. The ion mine falls away from your starship as you race away from the proton torpedo. A moment later, the mine detonates, destroying the torpedo in a massive explosion. You may proceed.

If your adventure# is less than 6, subtract the difference from your AP total. The ion mine is released from your starship, but it fails to blow up the proton torpedo. Proceed to blast the proton torpedo (below).

To blast the proton torpedo: Roll the 20-dice to target your laser cannons on the incoming warhead and fire. If targeting is one of your talents, your roll# + your skill# + your vehicle's weaponry# + 2 is your adventure#. If targeting is not one of your talents, your roll# + your skill# + your vehicle's weaponry# is your adventure#.

If your adventure# is equal to or more than 14, add the difference to your AP total. You shoot the torpedo and it detonates in a thunderous explosion. You may proceed.

If your adventure# is less than 14, subtract the difference from your AP total. Your blasts miss the warhead by millimeters. Although the proton torpedo is approaching fast, you still have another chance to fire. Roll the 20-dice again to fire once more at the incoming torpedo. Your new roll# + your skill# + your vehicle's weaponry# + 1 is your new adventure#.

If your new adventure# is equal to or more than 14, add the difference to your AP total. The proton torpedo is destroyed. You may proceed.

If your new adventure# is less than 14, subtract the difference from your AP total. Your vehicle has been hit — but luckily it survives. Your engine, however, is damaged. Subtract 1 from your vehicle's speed# and distance# for the rest of the adventure. You may then proceed.

The six-winged Bartokk fighter zooms by so close to your starship that you can see the three assassins in the cockpit. The Bartokks pull their fighter back in a tight loop, circling back to attack from the rear. A hail of crimson energy bolts spit out from the laser cannons mounted to each of the fighter's wings.

If your vehicle is the *Metron Burner,* you can use your pivoting quad laser cannons to return fire. If your vehicle is the Z-95

Headhunter, your laser cannons can only shoot what is in front of you, so you are unable to return fire at any starfighter that attacks from behind.

Choose to return fire with your quad laser cannons (your vehicle must be the *Metron Burner*), raise your deflector shields, or take evasive action.

To return fire with your quad laser cannons: Your vehicle must be the *Metron Burner*. Roll the 10-dice to fire back at the Bartokk starfighter. If defense is one of your talents, your roll# + your weaponry# + your vehicle's weaponry# is your adventure#. If defense is not one of your talents, your roll# + your vehicle's weaponry# is your adventure#.

If your adventure# is equal to or more than 7, add the difference to your AP total. Firing your cannons at the Bartokk starfighter, you manage to drive back the enemy ship. The Bartokks are on the defense but they are intent on killing you. You angle your ship in pursuit of the six-winged fighter and proceed.

If your adventure# is less than 7, subtract the difference from your AP total. Your cannons jam! Proceed to raise your deflector shields (next page).

To raise your deflector shields: Roll the 10-dice to activate the ray shielding around your ship. Your roll# + your vehicle's stealth# is your adventure#.

If your adventure# is equal to or more than 7, add the difference to your AP total. Your deflector shields come up just in time to prevent two blasts of enemy fire from scoring direct hits. Your shields absorb the energy from the blasts as you turn your starship to confront the Bartokk starfighter. You may proceed.

If your adventure# is less than 7, subtract the difference from your AP total. A warning light indicates your ray shielding will take another ten seconds to come online. If you wait for the shields to come up, you might not survive. Proceed to take evasive action (below).

To take evasive action: Roll the 20-dice to fly in a zigzag pattern to avoid being hit by enemy fire. If navigation is one of your talents, your roll# + your navigation# + your vehicle's stealth# + 2 is your adventure#. If navigation is not one of your talents, your roll# + your navigation# + your vehicle's stealth# is your adventure#.

If your adventure# is equal to or more than 14, add the difference to your AP total. Your unpredictable flight path brings the Bartokk starfighter into your firing range. You may proceed.

If your adventure# is less than 14, subtract 3 AP from your AP total. Despite your zigzag maneuver, the Bartokk fighter stays on your tail. You'll have to try harder to shake the three Bartokks. Roll the 20-dice again to throw your ship into a tight spin. Your new roll# + your navigation# + your vehicle's stealth# + 1 is your new adventure#.

If your new adventure# is equal to or more than 14, add the difference to your AP total. The Bartokks become dizzy in their effort to pursue you. Before they can reorient themselves, you have their fighter in your sights. You may proceed.

If your new adventure# is less than 14, subtract the difference from your AP total. Go back to "Roll the 20-dice again to throw your ship into a tight spin" and repeat. When you manage to get the Bartokk starfighter within your sights, you may proceed.

You have the Bartokk starfighter in your weapon sights. Choose to fire a concussion missile or your laser cannons at the six-winged fighter.

To fire a concussion missile: Roll the 10-dice to launch a long missile at the Bartokk starfighter. Your roll# + your vehicle's weaponry# is your adventure#.

If your adventure# is equal to or more than 6, add the difference to your AP total. The concussion missile streaks away from your ship and strikes the Bartokk starfighter. Both the missile and the starfighter explode, spraying glittering debris in all directions. You may proceed.

If your adventure# is less than 6, subtract the difference from your AP total. You should have checked your vehicle's armaments before leaving Esseles. Your missile launcher is empty! Proceed to fire your laser cannons (below).

To fire your laser cannons: Roll the 20-dice to shoot deadly bolts of energy at the enemy starfighter. If targeting is one of your talents, your roll# + your skill# + your weaponry# + your vehicle's weaponry# is your adventure#. If targeting is not one of your talents, your roll# + your weaponry# + your vehicle's weaponry# is your adventure#.

If your adventure# is equal to or more than 15, add the difference to your AP total. Your laser cannons hammer at the Bartokk starfighter until it explodes. You may proceed.

If your adventure# is less than 15, subtract the difference from your AP total. You missed the starfighter, and the Bartokks throw their ship into a tight spin. The tailgunner's cannons are aimed right at you! Unless you destroy their ship, the Bartokks will surely defeat you. Roll the 20-dice again to fire again at the six-winged starfighter. Your new roll# + your weaponry# + your vehicle's weaponry# + 1 is your new adventure#.

If your new adventure# is equal to or more than 14, add 2 AP to your AP total. You fire energy bolts directly into the Bartokk starfighter's cockpit. The entire fighter appears to collapse on itself before it explodes in a shower of sparks and fiery smoke. The Bartokks are defeated and you may proceed.

If your new adventure# is less than 14, subtract the difference from your AP total. Go back to "Roll the 20-dice again to fire again at the six-winged starfighter" and repeat. When you have destroyed the Bartokk starfighter, you may proceed.

You angle your starship back toward the Bartokk freighter.

You have defeated three more Bartokk assassins. Add 75 AP to your AP total.

During your battle with the six-winged starfighter, the freighter neared the edge of an asteroid belt. Many of the asteroids are relatively small chunks of planetary debris, but some are much larger than your own vehicle.

As you approach the spike-covered freighter, you see a hatch open at the main cargo hold. From out of the hatch, three objects are released into space. At first, you think the freighter is jettisoning a few long pieces of metal scrap. This doesn't surprise you, since unethical pilots routinely dump their junk in space to lighten their load and increase speed. But when the released objects extend dartlike wings and begin to move in your direction, you realize the Bartokks have deployed something far more hazardous than space junk.

The objects are Trade Federation droid starfighters.

Rather than risk any more members of their hive, the Bartokks have decided to use the stolen starfighters against you. Droid starfighters are indeed droids, programmed to attack without fear or remorse. The three fighters assume a triangulated assault formation and zoom in for the kill.

Although your deflector shields are raised, they'll require more energy to protect you from these enemy fighters. Unfortunately, the only way you can increase shield power is to divert energy from your sublight engine, which will decrease your vehicle's speed.

The nearby asteroid belt presents a dangerous option. If you pour on the speed, you might be able to lose the fighters in the asteroid belt.

The lead droid starfighter fires red energy bolts at your vehicle. Choose to increase deflector shield power, fire at the lead droid starfighter, or fly into the asteroid belt.

To increase deflector shield power: Roll the 10-dice to channel energy from your engine to your shields. Your roll# + your skill# + 2 is your adventure#.

If your adventure# is equal to or more than 7, add the difference to your AP total. Your shield power increases and easily deflects the barrage of energy bolts fired by the three droid starfighters. Unexpectedly, two starfighters break away from the formation while the lead prepares to ram your ship. Proceed to fire at the lead droid starfighter (below).

If your adventure# is less than 7, subtract the difference from your AP total. The energy bolts are coming at you too fast. You won't be able to increase power to your shields in time. Proceed to fly into the asteroid belt (next page).

To fire at the lead droid starfighter: Roll the 10-dice to train your laser cannons on the foremost fighter. Your roll# + your weaponry# + your vehicle's weaponry# is your adventure#.

If your adventure# is equal to or more than 8, add the difference to your AP total. Your cannons find their mark and the lead droid starfighter splinters into a million pieces. The two other droid starfighters keep their distance to avoid the explosion. You may proceed.

If your adventure# is less than 8, subtract the difference from your AP total. You miss the lead starfighter while enemy fire pounds at your weakening deflector shields. You must fly into the asteroid belt (below).

To fly into the asteroid belt: Roll the 20-dice to draw the three droid starfighters into the broad field of asteroids. Your roll# + your vehicle's speed# + your vehicle's stealth# is your adventure#.

If your adventure# is equal to or more than 13, add the difference to your AP total. You enter the asteroid belt at high speed. The three droid starfighters pursue you, but the lead starfighter collides with an asteroid and explodes. The other two starfighters keep their distance as you fly out of the asteroid belt. You may proceed.

If your adventure# is less than 13, subtract the difference from your AP total. Although you are navigating your starship through the thickly scattered asteroids as fast as possible, you cannot shake the three droid starfighters. Just ahead, you see two oblong asteroids suspended close to one another in space. Roll the 20-dice again to fly between the two asteroids. Your new roll# + your navigation# + your vehicle's stealth# + 2 is your new adventure#.

If your new adventure# is equal to or more than 14, add 3 AP to your AP total. You soar between the two oblong asteroids, and your quick passing causes them to rotate in opposing directions. The lead starfighter tries to pursue you but is smashed by the spinning asteroids. The other two starfighters keep their distance as you fly out of the asteroid belt. You may proceed.

If your new adventure# is less than 14, subtract the difference from your AP total. Go back to "Roll the 20-dice again to fly between the two asteroids" and repeat. After you have destroyed the lead droid starfighter and left the asteroid belt, you may proceed.

You are preparing to combat the two remaining droid starfighters when you remember an important fact about such weapons: droid starfighters don't have individual electronic brains. Each starfighter responds to commands transmitted by a remote central droid control unit. In this case, the control unit is doubtlessly located somewhere within the Bartokk freighter.

Although combating the two ships is an

option, you could try using your own starship's communications system to jam the signal that controls the droid starfighters. Destroying the triangular sensor dish on the freighter should also disable both droid starfighters.

Choose to jam the signal that controls the droid starfighters, shoot the Bartokk freighter's sensor dish, combat both droid starfighters using Power, or combat the droid starfighters one at a time.

To jam the signal that controls the droid starfighters: Roll the 10-dice to transmit a scattered burst of static across space. Your roll# + your skill# is your adventure#.

If your adventure# is equal to or more than 7, add the difference to your AP total. The static interferes with the signal that controls the droid starfighters. The two fighters spin out of control and smash into each other. You may proceed.

If your adventure# is less than 7, subtract the difference from your AP total. The starfighters are operating on a frequency that is protected from bursts of static. Proceed to shoot the Bartokk freighter's sensor dish (next page).

To shoot the Bartokk freighter's sensor dish: Roll the 20-dice to fire your laser cannons at the triangular dish. If targeting is one of your talents, your roll# + your weaponry# + your vehicle's weaponry# + 2 is your adventure#. If targeting is not one of your talents, your roll# + your weaponry# + your vehicle's weaponry# is your adventure#.

If your adventure# is equal to or more than 14, add the difference to your AP total. The triangular sensor dish explodes and the two starfighters spin off toward the asteroid belt. Both fighters crash into asteroids and you may proceed.

If your adventure# is less than 14, subtract the difference from your AP total. The reinforced sensor dish resists the initial attack from your cannons. Roll the 20-dice again to fire a more powerful blast. Your new roll# + your weaponry# + your vehicle's weaponry# + 3 is your new adventure#.

If your new adventure# is equal to or more than 15, add 4 AP to your AP total. The sensor dish tears away from the Bartokk freighter in a great explosion. You may proceed.

If your new adventure# is less than 14, subtract the difference from your AP total. It is possible the freighter is protected by a powerful deflector shield. Proceed to use Power to combat both droid starfighters or combat one droid starfighter at a time (below).

To combat both droid starfighters (using Power)*: Choose your Object Movement Power or Confusion Power. Roll the 20-dice to cause the two starfighters to collide. Your roll# + your Power# + your Power's high resist# + 1 is your adventure#.

If your adventure# is equal to or more than 13, add the difference to your AP total. The droid starfighters appear to wobble in space, then both crafts swing sharply and smash into each other at high speed. Starfighter fragments drift rapidly away at all angles from the collision site. You may proceed.

If your adventure# is less than 13, subtract the difference from your AP total. You don't have time to try using Power again. Proceed to combat one droid starfighter at a time (below).

*NOTE: This counts as one of three Power uses you are allowed on this adventure.

To combat one droid starfighter at a time: Roll the 10-dice to fire your cannons at the nearest starfighter. Your roll# + your weaponry# + your vehicle's weaponry# + 1 is your adventure#.

If your adventure# is equal to or more than 9, add the difference to your AP total. The nearest starfighter shatters, sending plastoid shrapnel and transparisteel splinters in every direction. Go back to "Roll the 10-dice to fire your cannons" and repeat. When you have destroyed both starfighters, you may proceed.

If your adventure# is less than 9, subtract the difference from your AP total. You missed! Roll the 10-dice again to fire once more at the elusive starfighter. Your new roll# + your weaponry# + your vehicle's weaponry# is your new adventure#.

If your new adventure# is equal to or more than 8, add 2 AP to your AP total. Your expert shooting destroys the droid starfighter. If one droid starfighter is still after you, go back to "Roll the 10-dice again to fire once more at the elusive starfighter" and repeat. When both starfighters are reduced to scrap metal, you may proceed.

If your new adventure# is less than 8, subtract the difference from your AP total. The starfighter evades your attack. Go back to "Roll the 10-dice again to fire once more at the elusive starfighter" and repeat. After you have defeated both droid starfighters, you may proceed.

Although you have destroyed three Federation droid starfighters, the Bartokks still have forty-seven of the fifty fighters stolen from Trinkatta's starship factory. Before the Bartokks have a chance to deploy another trio of fighters, you angle your vehicle back toward the freighter.

For destroying three droid starfighters, add 60 AP to your AP total.

The freighter's outer hull is protected by long metal spikes that release concentrated charges of energy. You want to board the freighter before any of the spikes have a chance to shoot your starship.

Boarding the Bartokk freighter will require two courses of action. First, you must destroy the freighter's deflector-shield generator, which is located under a small dome on top of the ship. After the shields are down, you must dock your ship to the freighter.

Proceed to destroy the freighter's deflector-shield generator.

To destroy the freighter's deflector-shield generator: Roll the 10-dice to shoot the small dome on top of the ship. Your roll# + your weaponry# + your vehicle's weaponry# is your adventure#.

If your adventure# is equal to or more than 9, add the difference to your AP total. Your cannons spit laser fire at the small dome until it shatters. The Bartokk freighter's shields drop and you may proceed to dock your ship to the freighter (below).

If your adventure# is less than 9, subtract 4 AP from your AP total. Before you can fire at the dome, one of the freighter's long spikes shoots a jarring bolt of energy at your vehicle. Another spike begins to glow bright green, preparing to launch another energy bolt. Roll the 20-dice to increase power to your deflector shields. Your new roll# + your skill# is your new adventure#.

If your new adventure# is equal to or more than 12, add 2 AP to your AP total. Your shield strength increases just in time to prevent the energy bolt from ravaging your vehicle. Now you must try again to attack the freighter's defenses. Go back to "Roll the 10-dice to shoot the small dome" and repeat this confrontation. When you have shattered the small dome on top of the freighter, you may proceed to dock your ship to the freighter (below).

If your new adventure# is less than 12, subtract 2 AP from your AP total. Go back to "Roll the 20-dice to increase power to your deflector shields" and repeat. After you have strengthened your own shields and destroyed the dome on top of the freighter, you may proceed to dock your ship to the freighter (below).

To dock your ship to the freighter: Roll the 10-dice to attach your vehicle to the same port that was previously occupied by the Bartokk starfighter. Your roll# + your navigation# + your skill# is your adventure#.

If your adventure# is equal to or more than 9, add the difference to your AP total. The docking was a success. Your vehicle's landing gear clamps on to the outside of the Bartokk freighter, linking the two ships at the freighter's docking port tube. You may proceed.

If your adventure# is less than 9, subtract the difference from your AP total. You nearly collide with drifting debris from the freighter's shattered deflector-shield generator. Roll the 10-dice again to try docking again. Your new roll# + your navigation# + your skill# + 1 is your new adventure#.

> *If your new adventure# is equal to or more than 9*, add the difference to your AP total. Your vehicle draws close to the Bartokk freighter's outer hull, then locks on to the freighter's docking port. You may proceed.

> *If your new adventure# is less than 9*, subtract the difference from your AP total. There's still too much debris floating around. Go back to "Roll the 10-dice again to try docking again" and repeat. After your vehicle is secured to the freighter, you may proceed.

You exit your vehicle and enter the Bartokk freighter's octagonal docking port tube. An eight-sided hatch is built within a thick plastoid frame at the end of the tube. If you are going to learn the freighter's destination, retrieve the prototype hyperdrive engine, and rescue the captured Chup-Chup, you must pass through this hatch.

The hatch is locked. You pass your hand over an illuminated control panel to open the hatch, but your non-Bartokk genetic makeup activates an anti-intruder security system.

A hissing sound alerts you to an invisible gas being pumped into the docking port tube. The gas is lethal. You must open the hatch before the poison fumes reach you.

Choose to open the hatch using Power, hot-wire the hatch's lock, or use your weapon to break through the hatch.

To open the hatch (using Power)*: Choose your Object Movement Power. Roll the 20-dice to unbolt the hatch's locking mechanism. Your roll# + your Power# + you Power's low-resist# is your adventure#.

> *If your adventure# is equal to or more than 11,* add the difference to your AP total. You hear the locking bolts slide out of the hatch and back into the walls. The hatch opens and you may proceed.

If your adventure# is less than 11, subtract 5 AP from your AP total. The presence of poison gas in the docking port tube makes you nervous. You must remain calm. Roll the 20-dice again. If calm is one of your talents, your roll# + your Power# + 3 is your adventure#. If calm is not one of your talents, your new roll# + your Power# + 1 is your new adventure#.

> *If your new adventure# is equal to or more than 12,* add 2 AP to your AP total. The hatch opens and you step out of the docking port tube. You may proceed.

> *If your new adventure# is less than 12,* subtract the difference from your AP total. You are unable to concentrate. Proceed to hot-wire the hatch's lock or use your weapon (below).

*NOTE: This counts as one of three Power uses you are allowed on this adventure.

To hot-wire the hatch's lock: Roll the 10-dice to manually override the illuminated control panel to open the octagonal hatch. If repair is one of your talents, your roll# + your knowledge# + your skill is your adventure#. If repair is not one of your talents, your roll# + your skill# is your adventure#.

If your adventure# is equal to or more than 7, add the difference to your AP total. The control panel is easily bypassed. The hatch opens and you may proceed.

If your adventure# is less than 7, subtract the difference from your AP total. The Bartokks' control panel is burglar-proof. The poison gas is rapidly filling the dock port tube. Proceed to use your weapon to break through the hatch (below).

To use your weapon to break through the hatch: Choose your weapon. Roll the 10-dice to target the hatch. Your roll# + your weaponry# + your weapon's close-range# is your adventure#.

If your adventure# is equal to or more than 8, add the difference to your AP total. You successfully carve or blast a hole through the octagonal hatch. Entering the freighter, you may proceed.

If your adventure# is less than 8, subtract 2 AP from your AP total. Using your weapon, you have made the hatch buckle within its octagonal frame, but now your weapon needs to recharge. A single well-placed kick to the hatch should knock it out of its frame and into the freighter. A strong individual or a good jumper should be able to launch a good kick. Roll the 10-dice again to kick in the hatch. If strength or jumping is one of your talents, your new roll# + your strength# + 2 is your adventure#. If strength or jumping is not one of your talents, your new roll# + your strength# is your new adventure#.

NOTE: If you injured your leg in a previous confrontation, subtract 2 from your adventure#.

If your new adventure# is equal to or more than 7, add the difference to your AP total. You kick the hatch in and follow the broken pieces into the freighter. You may proceed.

If your new adventure# is less than 7, subtract the difference from your AP total. You need to try another kick. Go back to "Roll the 10-dice again to kick in the hatch" and repeat. When the hatch is open, you may proceed.

As soon as the hatch opens, a massive whooshing sound bursts from the docking port tube, and you feel the air whip by you as if you've suddenly been caught in a strong wind. The Bartokks don't want their own freighter to be filled with poison gas, so an automatic safety feature has kicked in, suctioning the gas out of the docking tube and into space. Seconds later, the gas is ejected and the air becomes still.

You have successfully boarded the Bartokk freighter. Add 50 AP to your AP total.

With extreme caution, you move forward into the Bartokk freighter. You find yourself in a dark corridor that runs the length of the ship. You look to your left and right. Steam rises from ventilation slats in the metal floor, creating a damp, whispy haze that impairs your ability to see either end of the corridor. You guess that the Bartokks' bulbous, insectoid eyes don't require much light to find their way around on the ship.

The corridor is unusually quiet. The only thing you can hear is the steady, mechanical hum of the sublight engines, coming from the main engine room at the left end of the corridor.

Since you breached their security system in the docking port tube, the Bartokks must know you are on board. You are considering where to begin your search for the captured Chup-Chup when you see a shadowy figure moving toward you from the engine room area. The figure is clinging to the corridor's ceiling.

A quick glance to your right reveals that a second figure is moving toward you, crawling along the grilled floor from the outer end of the corridor. You realize you are trapped between two Bartokk assassins.

Since Chup-Chup is still onboard, retreating to your own starship is not an option. You must combat these assassins.

Choose to combat both assassins at once or one at a time. If you choose to combat both assassins at once, choose whether or not to use Power.

To combat both assassins at once (using Power): Choose your Confusion Power. Roll the 20-dice to create a situation which will cause the two Bartokks to attack each other. Your roll# + your Power# + your Power's mid-resist# + 1 is your adventure#.

If your adventure# is equal to or more than 14, add the difference to your AP total. In the dark corridor, the two Bartokks lash out at each other with their own weapons. You don't have to worry about them anymore. You may proceed.

If your adventure# is less than 14, subtract the difference from your AP total. The two Bartokks defy your attempt to make them fight each other. Proceed to combat both assassins at once, without Power (below).

*NOTE: This counts as one of three Power uses you are allowed on this adventure.

To combat both assassins at once (without Power): Choose your weapon. Roll the 10-dice to attack the two Bartokks with a swift, singular action. Your roll# + your weaponry# + your weaponry's mid-range# is your adventure#.

If your adventure# is equal to or more than 8, add the difference to your AP total. As the two Bartokks close in, you wait until they are both within range of your weapon. Your expert use of weaponry brings down the two assassins before they can attack in return. The two Bartokks are defeated and you may proceed.

If your adventure# is less than 8, subtract the difference from your AP total. Just as it appears both Bartokks are within range of your weapon, they suddenly move away from one another. You miss your chance to defeat them at the same time. Proceed to combat one assassin at a time (below).

To combat one assassin at a time: Choose your weapon. Roll the 20-dice to target the assassin to your left. Your roll# + your weaponry# + your weapon's close-range# is your adventure#.

If your adventure# is equal to or more than 13, add the difference to your AP total. The first assassin is felled. Go back to "Roll the 20-dice to target the assassin" and repeat. When you have defeated the second assassin, you may proceed.

If your adventure# is less than 13, subtract the difference from your AP total. The Bartokk slips into the shadows of the corridor and you miss. Roll the 20-dice again to attack further. Your new roll# + your weaponry# + your weapon's close-range# + 1 is your new adventure#.

If your new adventure# is equal to or more than 13, add 3 AP to your AP total. The

Bartokk assassin is downed by your weapon. If you have not yet set upon the second assassin, go back to "Roll the 20-dice again to attack further" and repeat. After the two assassins are defeated, you may proceed.

If your new adventure# is less than 13, subtract the difference from your AP total. The assassin dodges your attack and prepares to slay you. Go back to "Roll the 20-dice to attack further" and repeat. When both Bartokk assassins are felled by your weapon, you may proceed.

Two more assassins are out of commission. How many does that leave? If the two Bartokks in the corridor were able to telepathically alert their comrades of your presence, surviving Bartokks might be preparing to attack you.

One of the fallen assassins grips a pistol that packs a stun net charge. Such a weapon might be helpful if you run into more Bartokks. You take the pistol and secure it to your own weapons belt.

The other Bartokk clasps a device used to control a slaving collar. It's possible the assassins have forced Chup-Chup to wear a slaving collar, restraining him within the confines of the freighter.

You should be able to use the slaving-collar control to locate Chup-Chup. Otherwise, you must rely on your own tracking skills to find the captive Talz.

To find Chup-Chup, choose to use your instinct, use Power, or use the slaving-collar control as a tracking device.

To use your instinct to track Chup-Chup: Roll the 10-dice to search for any sign of the hostage Talz. If your talents include tracking or scent detection, your roll# + your knowledge# + 3 is your adventure#. If your talents do not include tracking or scent detection, your roll# + your knowledge# + 1 is your adventure#.

If your adventure# is equal to or more than 7, add the difference to your AP total. There are many Bartokk footprints on the corridor floor, but you quickly find Chup-Chup's unmistakable prints. You also pick up the Talz's scent. Chup-Chup's footprints and scent lead to the main cargo hold. You may proceed.

If your adventure# is less than 7, subtract the difference from your AP total. Your tracking abilities are hampered by the steam rising from the floor. Proceed to use the slaving-collar control as a tracking device (below).

To locate Chup-Chup (using Power)*:
Choose your Find Power. Roll the 20-dice to find Chup-Chup. Your roll# + your Power# + your Power's mid-resist# is your adventure#.

If your adventure# is equal to or more than 12, add the difference to your AP total. Chup-Chup is in the main cargo hold! You may proceed to save him.

If your adventure# is less than 12, subtract the difference from your AP total. You can't locate Chup-Chup. Try using the slaving-collar control as a tracking device (below).

*NOTE: This counts as one of three Power uses you are allowed on this adventure.

To use the slaving-collar control as a tracking device: Roll the 20-dice to locate the transmitting frequency for the slaving collar. Your roll# + your skill# + 1 is your adventure#.

If your adventure# is equal to or more than 12, add the difference to your AP total. According to the hand-held control, the slaving-collar and its wearer are located in the main cargo hold. You may proceed.

If your adventure# is less than 12, subtract 15 AP from your AP total. You have accidentally transmitted a signal that causes the control to shock you. It was only a temporary jolt, but it has shaken you up. Subtract 1 from your skill# for the rest of this adventure. Roll the 20-dice again to fine tune the controls of the hand-held device. Your new roll# + your skill# + 3 is your new adventure#.

If your new adventure# is equal to or more than 11, add the difference to your AP total. The device reveals that Chup-Chup is being held in the main cargo hold. You may proceed.

If your new adventure# is less than 11, subtract the difference from your AP total. You haven't tuned the device to the proper frequency. Go back to "Roll the 20-dice again to fine tune the controls" and repeat. When you have located Chup-Chup, you may proceed.

You walk up the corridor and enter the main cargo hold. Although there isn't any evidence of Chup-Chup, you have located the Trade Federation droid starfighters.

Like cave-dwelling winged rodents, the droid starfighters dangle upside down from a rack secured to the ceiling. The fighters have their wings folded up in their transport mode. Even at rest, the starfighters are a menacing sight to behold.

But the cargo hold is hardly filled to capacity. A quick count confirms there are only twenty-two droid starfighters. Because you destroyed only three droid starfighters in combat, you wonder what has happened to the remaining twenty-five Trade Federation fighters.

Searching for Chup-Chup within the cargo hold, you edge around a corner to find the hold's docking port. A magnetic field fills the rectangular port, separating the hold from outer space but allowing a spectacular view of the stars outside the freighter. You realize the three droid starfighters must have been deployed through this port.

A clanking sound causes you to turn to your left, and you find yourself staring at two Bartokks. Holding tools, they are working on what appears to be the prototype hyperdrive engine. The engine is clamped in place to a work table that's set near the hold's docking port.

Seeing you out of the corner of their bulbous eyes, the two assassins twitch their heads in your direction at the same time. They quickly drop their tools and reach for their crossbows.

To combat the two Bartokks, choose to use the stun net or open the docking port. If you choose to open the docking port, choose to open it with Power or by using one of your weapons.

To use the stun net on the two Bartokks: Roll the 10-dice to fire the launcher pistol. Your roll# + your skill# +1 is your adventure#.

If your adventure# is equal to or more than 7, add the difference to your AP total. Despite the fact that you've never fired a stun net before, you snag the two Bartokks with the first shot. The net unleashes a massive electric jolt as it snags the assassins, and they fall to the cargo room floor. You may proceed.

If your adventure# is less than 7, subtract the difference from your AP total. The pistol is designed for Bartokk claws and you are unable to fire it! Proceed to open the docking port using Power or using one of your weapons (next page).

To open the docking port (using Power)*:
Choose your Object Movement Power. Roll the
20-dice to activate the switch to drop the magnetic shield that protects the cargo hold from the
vacuum of space. Your roll# + your Power# +
your Power's mid-resist# + 1 is your adventure#.

*If your adventure# is equal to or more than
13,* add the difference to your AP total. The
shield drops and the two Bartokks are sucked
through the docking port and into space. Unfortunately, the powerful suction is also draw-
ing you out of the cargo hold! Proceed to
reactivate the magnetic field control switch
(next page).

If your adventure# is less than 13, subtract the
difference from your AP total. Proceed to
open the docking port using one of your
weapons (below).

*NOTE: This counts as one of three Power
uses you are allowed on this adventure.

**To open the docking port (using one of
your weapons):** Roll the 10-dice to target the
controls switch that deactivates the port's protec-
tive magnetic field. If targeting is one of your talents, your roll# + your weaponry# + your
weapon's far-range# + 2 is your adventure#. If
targeting is not one of your talents, your roll# +

your weaponry# + your weapon's far-range# is
your adventure#.

If your adventure# is equal to or more than 9,
add the difference to your AP total. You strike
the control switch and the magnetic field
opens. Unfortunately, you are also caught by
the powerful suction and find yourself being
lifted off the cargo hold floor and drawn
toward the open port. Unless you act fast, you
will be ejected into space! Proceed to reactivate the magnetic field control switch (below).

If your adventure# is less than 9, subtract the
difference from your AP total. Your shot
missed the control switch by one millimeter.
Go back to "Roll the 10-dice to target the controls switch" and repeat.

**To reactivate the magnetic field control
switch:** Roll the 10-dice to manually throw the
switch before you are dragged out of the cargo
hold and into space. If strength is one of your talents, your roll# + your strength# + your stealth#
is your adventure#. If strength is not one of your
talents, your roll# + your stealth# is your adven-
ture#.

If your adventure# is equal to or more than 6,
add the difference to your AP total. As you
near the port, you strike the control switch

and the magnetic field activates, sealing the port from space. You land on the cargo hold floor and may proceed.

If your adventure# is less than 6, subtract the difference from your AP total. Your muscles strain as you reach for the switch. Go back to "Roll the 10-dice to manually throw the switch" and repeat. After you have raised the magnetic field, you may proceed.

You hear a desperate pounding coming from the starboard airlock on the other side of the cargo hold. Airlocks are used to help spacers reacclimate to different environments, but in the wrong hands, the pressurized cabin can be a death chamber.

The circular airlock hatch is built into the thick plastoid wall. You run to the airlock and peer through a bubble-shaped transparisteel viewport, which offers a distorted view of the pressurized cabin's interior.

It's Chup-Chup. The Bartokks must have thrown him into the airlock.

Although you can't hear the young Talz, you see he is gasping for air and hammering his hairy fists against the walls. To the left of the airlock, a gauge indicates the sealed chamber is depressurizing. Unless you do something fast, Chup-Chup will die. You are reluctant to use any of your weapons to blast the airlock open because you might accidentally kill the poor Talz in the process.

There are ten buttons on the airlock control board. You are unfamiliar with the functions of each button, but if you hit the right one, you will free Chup-Chup. Proceed to open the airlock hatch.

To open the airlock hatch: Roll the 10-dice.

If you roll 1 or 2, the pressurization returns to normal within the airlock. Add 10 AP to your AP total. Chup-Chup is still trapped within the airlock, but at least he's breathing okay. To open the airlock hatch, roll again.

If you roll 3 or 4, the airlock begins to depressurize even faster. Subtract 10 AP from your AP total. Roll again, quickly.

If you roll 5 or 6, the airlock repressurizes, the hatch slides open, and Chup-Chup is released. Add 100 AP to your AP total. You may proceed.

If you roll 7 or 8, you activate one of the twenty-three droid starfighters. In walk mode, the droid starfighter lurches in your direction. You must deactivate the droid starfighter. Roll the 10-dice to push the button again. Your roll# + your skill# is your adventure#.

If your adventure# is equal to or more than 7, add the difference to your AP total. By pressing the correct button, you have made the droid retract its weapons and shut down. However, Chup-Chup is still trapped within the airlock. Go back to "To open the airlock hatch" and repeat.

If your adventure# is less than 7, subtract the difference from your AP total. The droid starfighter aims its laser cannons at you! Go back to "Roll the 10-dice to push the button again" and repeat.

If you roll 9 or 10, the airlock repressurizes, the hatch slides open, and Chup-Chup is released. Add 100 AP to your AP total. You may proceed.

Chup-Chup steps out of the airlock cabin. Despite his youth, the hairy Talz stands at 2.2 meters, which is slightly taller than his father. Unless you are Bama

Vook or Leeper, this is something of a surprise to you. Chup-Chup is very tall for his age.

If you are a Jedi, you give Chup-Chup a vocabulator so you can communicate and introduce yourself.

"Thank goodness you rescued me!" exclaims Chup-Chup. "I thought I was done for!"

"We're not out of this yet," you remind the Talz. "There are still Bartokk assassins at large, so we should get off of this freighter as soon as possible. I have a starship docked and ready to launch." You look at the prototype hyperdrive engine on the work table, then at the tall Talz. "I want to examine this prototype engine. Do you think you can carry it to our starship?"

Happy to help, Chup-Chup unclamps the cumbersome engine from the table and tucks it under one arm. Carrying the engine, the Talz follows you through the cargo hold and past the remaining Trade Federation droid starfighters.

"I was under the impression this freighter was carrying fifty droid starfighters when it left Esseles," you comment.

"It *was* carrying fifty starfighters," Chup-Chup notes. "But when the freighter entered space, another Bartokk freighter was waiting for us. The Bartokks transferred twenty-five starfighters to the second freighter."

"Transferred?" you echo. "Of course! That would have been the Bartokks' backup plan in case they were pursued from Esseles." Although you have little respect for the Bartokks, you admit they're cunning.

You lead the Talz out of the cargo hold and into the long, dark corridor. You return to the octagonal docking port tube and help Chup-Chup board the starship.

"Stay in the ship and wait for me," you order. "I still have to find out this freighter's destination."

You leave the docking port tube and walk up the corridor to the freighter's control room. Numerous lights glow and wink in the dim, filthy chamber. Thick cables dangle like mechanical vines from the ceiling, and a thin layer of moss covers some of the instruments. There isn't any sign of the surviving Bartokk crew. The freighter appears to be running on automatic.

Without warning, a Bartokk drops down from the ceiling.

The Bartokk carries four sharp gutting knives and he comes at you with immense speed and fury. If you hesitate, the Bartokk will open you up like a ripe blumfruit.

To combat the Bartokk, choose to use the stun net or one of your own weapons. If you used the stun net to snare the two Bartokks in the cargo hold, the stun net is no longer an option and you must use one of your own weapons.

To combat the Bartokk using the stun net: Roll the 10-dice to fire the launcher pistol. Your roll# + your skill# + 1 is your adventure#.

If your adventure# is equal to or more than 8, add the difference to your AP total. Despite the fact that you've never fired a stun net, you snag the Bartokk on the first shot. The net snags and stuns the assassin, and he falls to the control room floor. You may proceed.

If your adventure# is less than 8, subtract the difference from your AP total. Your lack of expertise with the stun net may be the end of you! You fire and miss the Bartokk. Proceed to use your own weapon (below).

To combat the Bartokk using one of your own weapons: Choose your weapon. Roll the 20-dice to draw your weapon and attack. Your roll# + your weaponry# + your weapon's mid-range# is your adventure#.

If your adventure# is equal to or more than 14, add the difference to your AP total. Although the Bartokk moves like lightning, you move faster. The Bartokk drops to the control room floor before he knows what hit him, and you may proceed.

If your adventure# is less than 14, subtract the difference from your AP total. The ferocious Bartokk drives you back across the control room. You must summon up all your strength to fight this assassin. Roll the 20-dice to knock the Bartokk to the floor. If strength or defense is one of your talents, your roll# + your strength# + 2 is your adventure#. If neither strength nor defense is one of your talents, your new roll# + your strength# is your new adventure#.

If your new adventure# is equal to or more than 11, add 5 AP to your AP total. Turning the tables on your attacker, you are victorious. You may proceed.

If your new adventure# is less than 11, subtract the difference from your AP total. The Bartokk won't give in that easily. Go back to "Roll the 20-dice to knock the Bartokk to the floor" and repeat. When you have defeated the Bartokk, you may proceed.

The battered Bartokk breathes in a harsh rasp. His insectoid body is propped up against a moldy console that houses the nav computer. From this computer, you should be able to learn the freighter's destination. However, it's possible the Bartokks have loaded the nav computer with false information. In that case, the destination might be drawn out of the Bartokk himself. Fortunately, the Bartokk is wearing a vocabulator, so you will be able to understand him.

If he talks.

To learn the freighter's destination, choose to use Power, trick the Bartokk, or access the nav computer.

To persuade the Bartokk to talk (using Power)*: Choose the Persuasion Power. Roll the 20-dice to ask the assassin where his freighter is headed. Your roll# + your Power# + your Power's low-resist# is your adventure#.

If your adventure# is equal to or more than 12, add the difference to your AP total. The captured Bartokk tells you the freighter is bound for the planet Corulag. You may proceed.

If your adventure# is less than 12, subtract the difference from your AP total. The strong-willed Bartokk resists your power and remains silent. Proceed to trick the Bartokk (below) or access the nav computer (next page).

*NOTE: This counts as one of three Power uses you are allowed on this adventure.

To trick the Bartokk: Roll the 10-dice to tell the Bartokk you already know his destination is the planet Kalarba. Your roll# + your charm# + 1 is your adventure#.

If your adventure# is equal to or more than 8, add the difference to your AP total. The Bartokk replies, "Kalarba? Ha! You're so wrong! We're bound for Corulag!" As soon as the words leave his mandibles, the Bartokk spews a flurry of angry words. He can't believe he revealed the freighter's destination so easily. You may proceed.

If your adventure# is less than 8, subtract 5 AP from your AP total. The Bartokk is smarter than he looks and remains silent. Roll the 10-dice again to try a different approach: you tell the captured assassin that the Trade Federation is on to him, and will kill him once the Bartokks reach their destination. Your new roll# + your charm# + 3 is your new adventure#.

> *If your new adventure# is equal to or more than 10,* add the difference to your AP total. "If they wanted to kill me, why would they wait until we reached Corulag?" he wonders aloud, then realizes his blunder. He has revealed the planetary location and you may proceed.

> *If your new adventure# is less than 10,* subtract the difference from your AP total. Subtract the difference to your AP total. You won't get a single word out of this Bartokk. Proceed to access the nav computer (below).

To access the nav computer: Roll the 10-dice to enter a destination query into the Bartokk navigational program. Your roll# + your knowledge# + your skill# is your adventure#.

If your adventure# is equal to or more than 8, add the difference to your AP total. According to the nav computer, the freighter is bound for the planet Corulag. Content with the information, you may proceed.

If your adventure# is less than 8, subtract the difference from your AP total. The nav computer responds that the Bartokks' destination is the planet Shrikstak. Since Shrikstak's sun went nova almost a year ago, you know this must be falsified information. Go back to "Roll the 10-dice to enter a destination query" and repeat. When you have learned the freighter's destination, you may proceed.

"You will not defeat the Bartokks," the assassin hisses through his mandibles. "Our assignment will be carried out no matter what you do!"

You have learned the Bartokk freighter's destination. Add 50 AP to your AP total.

"I already know about how you transferred twenty-five droid starfighters to a second Bartokk freighter," you reveal. "I'll make sure the ship never reaches its destination. Just wait until I turn you over to the authorities."

"I would sooner die than remain your hostage!" the Bartokk sneers. Suddenly, he twists his neck sharply and bites down. His mandible contains a quick-acting toxin that instantly kills the Bartokk.

The Bartokk freighter might contain too many booby traps to reprogram a new destination or allow its return to Esseles. To prevent the freighter and its cargo of twenty-two droid starfighters from reaching Corulag, you must destroy the entire ship.

You inspect the dead Bartokk's weapons. He happens to be carrying a proton grenade equipped with a timer. Activating the grenade in the control room could cause a chain reaction to blow up the freighter.

Setting the proton grenade is a two-step process. First, you must twist the grenade's arming mechanism, which will prime the grenade's battery to deliver a small electrical charge to the proton core.

Second, you press the activation plunger to start the timer.

You set the timer for a two-minute countdown. Proceed to twist the grenade's arming mechanism (below).

To twist the grenade's arming mechanism: Roll the 10-dice to prime the grenade's battery. Your roll# + your skill# + 1 is your adventure#.

If your adventure# is equal to or more than 8, add the difference to your AP total. The battery is primed. Proceed to press the activation plunger (below).

If your adventure# is less than 8, subtract the difference from your AP total. You twisted the mechanism in the wrong direction. Go back to "Roll the 10-dice to prime the grenade's battery" and repeat.

To press the activation plunger: Roll the 20-dice to start the grenade's timer. Your roll# + your skill# + your strength# is your adventure#.

If your adventure# is equal to or more than 15, add the difference to your AP total. Pressing the activation plunger, you begin the two-minute countdown to the freighter's destruction. You may proceed.

If your adventure# is less than 15, subtract 7 AP from your AP total. You didn't press the plunger hard enough. Roll the 20-dice again to press the activation plunger with more strength. If strength is one of your talents, your new roll# + your skill# + your strength# + 2 is your new adventure#. If strength is not one of your talents, your new roll# + your skill# + your strength# is still your new adventure#.

> *If your new adventure# is equal to or more than 14,* add the difference to your AP total. The timer is activated and you have two minutes to escape the freighter. You may proceed.

> *If your new adventure# is less than 14,* subtract the difference from your AP total. You almost set the timer at two seconds! Go back to "Roll the 20-dice again to press the activation plunger with more strength" and repeat. When you have pressed the plunger, you may proceed.

As the proton grenade ticks off the passing seconds, you run from the control room and race down the dark corridor. Your feet pound on the metal floor and the rising steam wets your face. You are almost at the octagonal docking port when you see a shadowy form slip out from the shadows.

It's the last Bartokk assassin. Each one of his four arms wields a different weapon: a gutting knife, a spear, a crossbow loaded with two poison-tipped arrows, and a stun net. Unexpectedly, he drops all the weapons and lets them fall to the corridor floor. At first, you think the Bartokk is offering his surrender, but as he lurches forward, you realize he has something else in mind.

The Bartokk wants to take you apart with his own bare claws.

Choose to evade or combat the last Bartokk. If you choose combat, choose to combat him with your bare hands or use your weapon.

To evade the last Bartokk: Roll the 10-dice to jump past the Bartokk and into the docking port tube. If jumping is one of your talents, your roll# + your strength# + your stealth# is your adventure#. If jumping is not one of your talents, your roll# + your stealth# is your adventure#.

If your adventure# is equal to or more than 7, add the difference to your AP total. You enter the docking port tube and enter your starship before the Bartokk can follow. You may proceed.

If your adventure# is less than 7, subtract the difference from your AP total. The Bartokk steps in front of the docking port tube and blocks your access. Proceed to combat the Bartokk using your bare hands or your weapon (below).

To combat the Bartokk with your bare hands: Roll the 10-dice to level the Bartokk with a devastating chop to his insectoid neck. If your talents include defense or strength, your roll# + your strength# + 2 is your adventure#. If your talents do not include defense or strength, your roll# + your strength# + 1 is your adventure#.

If your adventure# is equal to or more than 8, add the difference to your AP total. Your attack knocks the Bartokk out cold. He collapses to the corridor floor while you enter the docking port tube to your starship. You may proceed.

If your adventure# is less than 8, subtract the difference from your AP total. You must have been slightly out of your mind to think you could ever defeat a Bartokk barehanded. He grabs hold of you and begins to drool on your head. Proceed to combat the Bartokk using a weapon (below).

To combat the Bartokk using your weapon: Choose your weapon. Roll the 20-dice to target the last assassin. Your roll# + your weaponry# + your weaponry's close-range# + 1 is your adventure#.

If your adventure# is equal to or more than 15, add the difference to your AP total. Your weapon finds its mark. You step through the docking port tube and board your starship. You may proceed.

If your adventure# is less than 15, subtract 8 AP from your AP total. The swift Bartokk dodges your attack. You'll have to throw all of your strength into this fight. Roll the 20-dice again to attack the Bartokk. Your new roll# + your strength# + your weaponry# + your weaponry's close-range# is your new adventure#.

If your new adventure# is equal to or more than 17, add the difference to your AP total. The shattered assassin topples to the corridor floor. You board your starship and proceed.

If your new adventure# is less than 17, subtract the difference from your AP total. Go back to "Roll the 20-dice again to attack the Bartokk" and repeat. When you have defeated the assassin, you may proceed.

Stepping onto your starship, you shout, "Get us out of here, Chup-Chup! The freighter's going to explode in less than thirty seconds."

"But I'm not old enough to fly a starship," Chup-Chup whimpers.

You jump into the cockpit and grab the controls. You must blast away from the Bartokk freighter.

To blast away from the Bartokk freighter: Roll the 10-dice to fly at high speed away from the doomed freighter. Your roll# +

your navigation# + your vehicle's speed# is your adventure#.

If your adventure# is equal to or more than 8, add the difference to your AP total. Your starship tears away from the freighter at the last possible second. You may proceed.

If your adventure# is less than 8, subtract the difference from your AP total. Go back to "Roll the 10-dice to fly at high speed" and repeat. When you have launched away from the spike-covered ship, you may proceed.

Within the Bartokk freighter, the proton grenade detonates just as your starship breaks off into space. Suddenly, the entire freighter erupts in a violent explosion that sends a small shock wave across space.

"Where to now?" Chup-Chup asks from behind your seat. "We're not going after the other Bartokk freighter, are we?"

"Not yet," you say as you steer the starship back toward Esseles. "Our first stop is Trinkatta Starships to check on our friends. If there's any chance of stopping that other freighter, we'll need all the help we can get!"

You have rescued Chup-Chup, retrieved the prototype hyperdrive engine, learned the Bartokk freighter's destination, and destroyed the freighter. Add 300 AP to your AP total.

To read the end of this adventure, please turn to page 88 of your Star Wars Adventures novel, *The Bartokk Assassins*.